Eco Asylum
1 St Paul St, Suite 303A
St Catharines, ON
L2R7L4
(289)929-6158
Ordering Information:
Quantity sales. Special discounts are available on quantity purchases by corporations, associations, and others. For details, contact the publisher at the address above.

Orders by U.S. trade bookstores and wholesalers. Please contact Eco Asylum:
Tel: (289) 929-6158 or www.ecoasylum.com

Schools and Libraries: Please contact Eco Asylum tel (289) 929-6158 or fill out the contact form at www.ecoasylum.com

Printed simultaneously in Canada and the United States of America. For translations, transcriptions, audio books and braille please fill out the contact form at www.ecoasylum.com

This novel is a work of fiction and entirely the construction of the author. Any resemblance to persons living or dead is entirely coincidental.

SPOOKY

STORIES

FOR KIDS

MK BELL

LOCKED UP

All of the kids in Brighton knew about the old school in the woods, but almost nobody went there. it was a really hard ride, for one thing. You had to go all the way to the end of Quentin's street and then turn your bike into the woods. The path to get there wasn't at all straight: there were twisted-up trees on both sides and it was mostly overgrown with weeds.

You could break your neck going through those woods. Maybe that was why they had closed the school and built the new one in the center of town. The school Quentin went to had brand new windows, red laquered doors, and two large gymnasiums. Quentin thought about it, missing it as he looked into the woods.

They didn't just look creepy, he realized. They felt scary, too. Looking into those woods, you felt like something with long, cold fingers had gripped you hard by he shoulder, its nails digging into your chest.

Nelson and Adam didn't care. They stood in his yard, looking into the woods, punching eachother on the shoulder and chuckling loudly.

"Come on man, you've gotta do it. It's a dare."

"I don't have to do anything."

"Then you're chicken!" Nelson shouted.

"No jam!" Adam wailed.

In Brighton, "no jam" was the worst thing you could say to anybody. It was worse than a dare, and stronger than chicken. If you didn't do it, everybody at school would laugh at you for the rest of the year.

"He's all peanut butter!" Nelson had the loudest voice in school. At lunch in the gym, you could hear him talking over everybody else. Everyone at school always knew what he was talking about.

Which meant that on Monday, they would all know Quentin James had no jam. He had to do it.

"I don't have a flashlight?" he tried.

"Aw, c'mon. It aint that dark out. You'll be back before it gets dark. It's not like you have to stay overnight in the old school."

"He should have to stay overnight."

"Good point, Adam." Nelson's pale face was turning red in the cheeks, red and raw. The two of them looked like tweedle-dee and tweedle-dum, shaking bellies hanging out the bottom of black and white striped shirts.

"I'm going," Quentin shouted, already getting on his bike. "How I ended up having to take a challenge from these neanderthals, I will never know."

They probably said something back, but he was already flying over the trail on his bike, legs pushing the pedals as fast as they could in the summer sun. He had to get there fast, and get back even faster.

He rode through the woods, scared the whole time that he was going to hit a rock and go flying off his bike. It was pretty close a few times, but Quentin was a good rider and his bike was brand new. The tires had just been pumped this morning. Even so, the long and bumpy trail with its sharp rocks and crazy turns sent him flying up into the air a few times, pedalling in the air and waiting to fall back into his seat.

When he came to the top of the hill, he saw it.

The woods were creepy, but the school was even worse. The weeds that looked green in the woods looked black and toxic wrapped around the school's dark brown brick walls. Water stains came halfway down the walls from the roof, and the window bars still hung half off of their screws. Trash littered the yard at the end of a very thin dirt trail that ended at a long fence. Would he even be able to get through?

"I could lie, and tell them I did it. I don't have to go in."

Goosebumps stood up on his arms. That sounded like a pretty good idea.

Until his phone rang.

Adam. He knew before he hit the answer button.

"We've been waiting for an HOUR, man! Are you there yet?"

Quentin tossed the strands of long blond hair out of his face and checked the time on his phone. "It's been fifteen minutes. Chill."

"Get it on video, or it doesn't count."

Adam hung up before he could argue.

"No jam. No jam." He reminded himself.

He pushed off and let himself fly down the trail, the way he had learned to do when he was little. It was easy. All you had to do was let go. It was being afraid that messed you up. If you got scared going down a hill, you might try to slam on the brakes and go flying over the handlebars. You might tense up and end up with your face on the pavement, split lipped and headed for a hospital.

But if you let yourself coast, everything turned out fine.

At the last second, Quentin spun his bike hard to the left and threw himself into the chain-link fence, which caught him as comfortably as a mattress. If he couldn't get in, it wouldn't be his fault, right?

The gate opened on its own. Weird. It must be left over from when the school was still running. Pressure plates under the grass, or something.

Without warning, a bell sounded a loud and blaring peal. He almost jumped three feet in the air at the sound of it, and looked around wildly to figure out where it came from. A bell? Out here?

Holding his chest to keep his heart in, Quentin saw the large, round object on the side of the school. An old fashioned school bell, and the hammer was vibrating against the side. Why would that thing still work?

"I just have to go inside."

He put them in the locker.

That wasn't a school bell! Quentin ran toward the school, away from the sound of a voice whispering in his ear, one that seemed made-up as soon as he thought about it, and he ran smack into the dark wooden front door.

This place didn't look so great, and for all he knew it had looked even worse when there were kids here. Thinking about his modern school with its red laquered doors and brand new baseball diamond, he felt sorry for them.

He felt sorry for himself.

At the last second, he remembered to pull up Vidchat and add the tweedles to a room. Focusing the camera on his face, he put on his bravest voice.

"Told you I could do it." He leaned up against the dark brick, trying to seem cool

He put them in the locker.

The phone dropped from his hand as fast as he'd picked it up, flipping over twice in the air before it landed face down in the muck beneath his feet. Of course.

"What happened? I don't see anything!"

"I think he dropped the phone!"

The sound of the two boys laughing echoed in the silent grove as Quentin picked up his phone and wiped it on his shorts. It was a good thing there wasn't still a school full of kids here to stare at the weird skinny blond kid in his striped polo and oversized khaki shorts. His shoes were covered in muck, and he had no idea how to explain that to his mom.

Right now, he had bigger problems.

"Guys, I think there's something here." He saw their round faces through a film of something wet and brown. A wad of gum was stuck to the side of his screen, and he carefully pried it off. Yup. His mom was going to kill him. "A ghost."

"Okay, Quentin."

"Yeah, right."

"I'm serious. It keeps saying the same thing over and over. He put them in the locker."

"Alright look, Quentin. I wasn't going to tell you this," Adam started. Nelson put a hand on his chest, eyes open wide in shock. "Don't tell him. He's already scared enough."

"He deserves to know!" Adam looked into the camera, his face taking up the whole screen as he moved his phone closer. "Before you moved here, they closed the school down. You know that, but you don't know why. We do. We were there."

"Why did they close the school?" Something cold ran up Quentin's spine, icy fingers from the grave.

"Don't you know about the dead kids?"

Nelson grabbed the phone. "Look, we NEED you. Just remember that. If you don't go into that school and fix this, bad things are going to happen. Kids are going to be hurt. They might even.."

"There was a janitor working for the school, and we all thought he was really nice. He'd bring cookies and candy. He watched out for us. But one day he just went crazy. He started taking kids. And nobody knew where they were until...until the principal went down the stairs and into the basement. Do you know what he found?"

"The kids?"

Adam nodded solemnly. "In locker 401b. Right beside the furnace. It was pretty easy to figure out what he was planning to do. Maybe he'd already done it. But the kids weren't dead."

"They weren't alive, either," Nelson said, grabbing the phone. "And every year on the anniversary of their death, the kids come back. They look just like you and me. Except..."

"You don't want to know what except is. Look, man, those kids are looking for something. We need you to stop them this time...before they get out."

"Me? Why me?"

"Why not you?"

The screen went full black, and he shook it, smacked it, trying to restore the picture. When it did come back the screen was blue and purple. A kid's face climbed out of the murk like a person seen through fog on a dark day.

The sound came from his phone this time.

He put them in the locker.

This time when he dropped his phone, he left it in the muck. Good luck to the kid who found it! He would rather have no phone then ever pick up the haunted one again.

Fast as he could, he ran toward the fence and his bike, without looking up until he almost ran into them. At the last second, he rocked back on his ankles because they were there, at the fence. Hundreds of them. A crowd of kids with razor sharp teeth and hands like claws, staring at him. Their eyes didn't look human. They looked blank, like the pages of a notebook that hadn't been written on yet. They were drooling and snarling. He was scared they would eat him.

Instead, they turned away from him and began to walk through the open gate, taking the path toward town. One of them turned back for a second and he could have sworn he saw it close one eye to wink. Like they were friends sharing a secret joke.

"Oh no, oh no, oh no! What am I supposed to do?!" Quentin reached up and pulled at the long strands of his hair, face arranged in a mask of fear. He HAD to go into that school! He HAD TO.

He put them in the locker. He took them away, and he put them in the locker.

"I know that! I'm going!"

Then he thought of riding on his bike. Of going down a steep hill, feet pointed out and hands barely gripping the handlebars, until the last second, when he had to stop. He thought of the way fear messed you up sometimes: when you tried to put the brakes on and ended up flying over the handles, or your muscles seized up and you faceplanted on the ground.

He remembered all the split lips and ripped clothes and dropped phones being afraid had gotten him, and he made up his mind. Quentin James was not going to be afraid. He was going into that school.

Besides, what was in front of him was way more scary.

He ran back toward the school, slamming the gate behind him as he went. One of the kid monsters turned back when it closed, but only for a seccond. They were on a mission, and thank goodness, it didn't involve him. Not right now.

The front door was locked, so he ran around the school trying all of the others. None of them opened by magic, and why would they? He had a feeling they only opened for the kids. The ones who lived there.

The ones who would be there forever.

The window.

About halfway up the blackened brick, a window was standing open, maybe left that way by some teacher on her last day, ready for summer vacation to start and the new school to be built. All of the windows had big ledges, big enough to put your foot on. Gripping the lowest one with his fingers, Quentin swung himself sideways onto the ledge. One ledge at a time, he made it up to the open window.

He expected more monsters, chalk that wrote by itself, or ghostly students sitting in scratched desks covered with cobwebs. Instead, he hang dropped feet first into a large open room that still smelled of wood and laquer and chalk dust. The desks were long gone, maybe stored in some baseement. Or maybe, he shuddered, they were the same ones the kids at his school used.

Something was written on the chalkboard, and he moved closer to read it.

A poem.

The kids of class 304b
got stuck by the clock
if you don't hurry you will too
tock, tick, tock.

Every boy and girl
and the teacher too
starved to death in their desks
hurry, or you will too.

What the?

Hurry.

Run.

He ran out of the classroom and down the shallow stairs, not paying attention to anything around him. Just thinking about that hill, about flying down it, about getting out of this awful school before...before WHAT?

They starved to death.

"Adam was wrong."

He put them in the locker. The basement. Go to the basement. He took them and he put them in the locker.

"The person who listens to the creepy voice in a scary movie usually dies!" he yelled, his voice as loud as Nelson's in the forever quiet school, and only quiet answered. Quiet, and something else. Not a sound, but a feeling. He FELT the school take a deep breath and hold it in, and himself with it.

Hurry. Hurry.

He ran down several flights of stairs toward the place where the locker was supposed to be, the one where he kept the kids, the ones that died.

Them, and the kids from class 304b.

At the bottom of the stairs, propelled forward by fear and wanting to do the right thing, Quentin nearly fell through the door. The basement was dark and grey, and his feet slipped in something gross on the floor. Not even the auxilliary lights shone down here, and he silently wished his phone was in his hand right now.

Why hadn't he brought it, at least for the flashlight?

Something reached out of the darkness, taking him by the wrist as his stomach jumped into his throat and he felt about to vomit. A cold, white hand, attached to a pale, young girl. She had blonde hair, like his, and her eyes were black pools in the dark.

"I've been trying to open it." There were tears in her voice, and hair hung in straight sticks to the middle of her back. She wore brown corduroy pants with a grey and red striped top. That was all he could see as she disappeared into the darkness, pulling him along. Things lit up around her, like she glowed. At least a little. She stopped, and pointed. "I don't know the combination."

"How would I know it?"

She looked at him, and it was impossible to tell what expression was on her face behind those dark eye holes. Her head tilted to one side and there was a little smile on her face.

"It's yours."

Impossible.

She shoved him toward the locker, nudging him closer to its rust and peeling paint. Her hands were colder than cold, and he wanted her to stop touching him. It seemed like the fastest way to get rid of her was to dial his combination into the lock.

He spun the rusted lock once to the left, and then stopped at the number 34. Twice to the right, and around again to 25. Twice more left. Zero. He pulled.

Pulled again. Harder this time.

Nothing.

"I don't know it. You see? I don't know the combination to this thing. Please let me go!'

He was frightened now: of the school and the pale bright girl, and what his friends would think if he peed his pants. He could already feel it threatening, and wanted to just get out of here and find a bathroom. In a day or two he could forget this. It would be a bad dream.

"Not that one. Your other one."

Other one?

He tried his birthdate. Nothing. His mom's, sisters. All his favorite numbers. His dog's birthday. The result was always the same, and his sense of dread grew. Putting a hand over his and a finger to his lips, she held him tightly, watching something only she could see until it passed.

She whispered, "The combination you stole from him right before they locked the school down. When they were searching for the janitor. You knew where he was all along, David. You know the combination. Please. Hurry. He's coming."

Who was David? Maybe...his old school! He hadn't tried that one yet. It was the only one. Maybe.

It already felt right. He spun the lock. Once to the right. Four. Twice to the left. Eight. Twice to the right.

Click.

Nothing.

"It's not working."

"Try it again. Try again. Hurry. Please."

"You're one of the kids, aren't you? The one he locked up in the locker. Why should I help you? I've seen scary movies. You'll probably do something awful if I help you."

"Please! It happens this way every time! You have to trust me! We're running out of time."

Fear. It gets you every time. It makes your hands shake, doesn't it? Even if the numbers are right. Just one click in the wrong direction.

He turned the lock again, and this time, it opened.

Food came spilling out of the locker. More than it could have held: chips and chocolate bars and cans and bottles of pop. Enough food to feed an army for a year.

"THIS is what the janitor locked up? Candy?"

"And toys. They're coming back," she said, looking up.

"I'm out of here!"

Quentin ran, faster than he ever had before, and had just time to get out the upstairs window before they came back, crowds and crowds of kid-zombies with glazed over eyes and razor sharp teeth. He didn't stop for his phone, or his bike. Fear took over and he ran into the woods, pale legs pumping fast, up and down, feet slapping the trail as he ran for home. Branches scraped his legs raw and red, but he didn't care.

He fell on his lawn, terror printed all over his face, just in time to catch the tweedles about to leave. They looked surprised to see him.

"What happened?" They shouted, big eyed, at the same time. "We were about to call the cops to go look for you!"

"Did you find any ghosts with unfinished business?"

"Candy," he gasped, out of breath, tired, and dirty.

"What?"

"The janitor...confiscated...their candy...not kids. It was...candy."

Nelson and Adam stared at him, mouths hanging open.

"I'd haunt him for that, too."

"I'd haunt him twice."

CANDY

When you choose your friends, it's important to know what kind of candy they like. If you don't choose wisely, then on Halloween night you might end up stuck with a bag full of chocolate bars and nobody to trade them with for candy corn.

Amy, Bradley, Jesse, Quinn, and Reginald P. Higgins III knew this. They had chosen wisely. Every Halloween night they went trick or treating together and divided up the candy so that everybody got exactly what they wanted.

Last Halloween, Amy was dressed as a dog. She painted freckles on her face and combed her long, blonde hair into two straight ponytails that looked like dog ears. Her mother helped her to sew a fun-fur suit that would be cute AND keep her warm outside. That was important for a hard-core trick-or-treater like Amy. A person had to start early, go home late, and trick or treat the houses with the MOST candy closest together, if a person expected to have enough candy corn stashed in the big drawer underneath her bed to last the ENTIRE YEAR. Which was exactly what Amy expected.

Bradley had covered his real freckles with smears of dirt, and Amy couldn't tell if he was supposed to be a Pirate or a hobo. He wasn't a big fan of candy, but he was big on pranks. Bradley would trade ANY-THING for a bag of pop rocks. He showed up first, and dropped his pillowcase on the chair in Amy's hall. "Did your mom buy any candy to give out?" he asked. His expression under all the dirt looked like a dog in a room full of meat, sniffing the air.

"Sorry. She's going to a party."

Bradley looked disappointed, but he perked right up when the rest of the kids came: Jesse, who was dressed as a cowgirl complete with the horse, high-fived her best friend when she came through the door. Reginald, who had come as an exchange student and stayed when his family moved to town, spoke in an even more posh British accent than usual. He was dressed in a pin-striped grey suit and a monacle. He had a tea saucer in one hand, and a cup in the other.

"Who are you supposed to be?" Bradley asked, loudly. He and Jesse were always loud, crazy, and super fun to be around. Without them, everything seemed like a boring adult party.

"I'm Caspar Milquetoast."

"You're weird."

"Woah, man, wicked!"

Bradley, Jesse, and Reginald were staring open-mouthed at Quinn's costume. He wore a long robe that seemed to stop far above his head, covering his face. He looked like an eight foot tall man.

"Wow, Quinn! You went all out! How did you get it to stand up so far above your head? Did your mom make the robe? How did you do the pattern?"

The black robe was covered in bright red swirls and loops, an abstract pattern that reminded her of rich people's curtains.

Quinn, who seemed almost not to have heard them, said "Candy."

"He's right! We're burning moonlight! Let's go!"

They ran out the door and into the quiet street, all of them standing on the sidewalk outside of Amy's house. They waited for IT to happen.

Reginald began the countdown, and then they all joined in: "Five...four....three....two...."

"Candy."

You weren't allowed to go trick-or-treating on Baker street until the streetlights turned on. There were groups of kids everywhere in the neighborhood who were waiting to hear the sound of the bulbs crackling a little, and then popping on, to see the faint light that meant they were on, and it was time to go!

"Candy."

What the heck was wrong with Quinn? But there was no time. They ran to the first house, yelling trick-or-treat as quickly as they could, and meeting on the lawn to discuss what they had gotten. How to divide it, who would get what. Important matters.

"Ugh, all I got was those stupid caramels our parents won't let us eat."

"Candy."

"Oh my gosh, fine! Here, Quinn! Nobody wants these anyway!"

Quinn reached up under the dark hood and his hand disappeared for a moment as he threw the candy in. The hand came back, but the caramels stayed gone.

"You like caramels now?"

Quinn nodded.

"I guess we can find somebody else to take the bags of chips."

"Candy. Candy Candy Candy."

"I get it! He's a candy monster! I get the head now, too. He must have his candy bag in there. That's genius! Can I borrow it next year, Quinn? Quinn?" But he was already at the next house.

And something was strange about his voice.

"He's fast! You coming, Amy?"

"You guys go ahead. I'll be there in a second. I just need

to check something first."

Amy took out her cell phone and dialled Quinn's house. His mother answered on the first ring. She sounded like she'd been running.

"Amy? Is that you? Is anything wrong?"

"I'm sorry, Mrs....Quinn's mom. I forgot your number was on the emergecy call list. We're okay. Nothings wrong. We're just leaving my house and on our way to yours. But...is Quinn okay?"

"Of course, sweetheart. He's just a little sick. He lost his voice today. Just between you and me, it was nice to have a little quiet around the house."

"Lost his voice?" But.... "But he's talking."

"Of course he is! Couldn't lose his voice all day, or he'd have been stuck eating whatever I wanted to cook for dinner. He's still a bit hoarse, but coming along fine."

"That explains it."

"Explains what?"

"Goodbye, Mrs. Quinn's mom!" Amy hung up the phone and ran to join her friends. She'd almost lost them (and her chance to trade candy) by standing too long at the corner yakking on her phone.

"Everything okay?"

"With me? Sure. I just had to call Quinn's mom to make sure he's okay. He sounds weird, doesn't he?"

Jesse grinned and shook out her red hair. "Oh, you mean the voice? Or him saying nothing but 'candy, candy, candy' this whole time?"

"Both. But it's fine. His mom says he just has a cold."

Krissy and Katie, the toddler twins, were dressed as matching pink kitties. Everybody knew that if you complimented their costumes you got twice as much candy, so the kids started exclaiming about how cute and adorable and fluffy they were. Katie smiled and dug her pudgy toddler-hand into a bowl full of candy, coming up with all sorts of treasures for the kids.

Each of them left with a handful or two of candy except Quinn, who didn't say they looked cute or adorable or fluffy-tailed at all. He just said;

"Candy."

By 8pm they were all exhausted. They had been out for more than two hours, walking and trick-or-treating, checking in at the designated houses along their neighborhood's safe trick-or-treating list as they went. Their bags had gotten heavier and heavier. Their legs had gotten more and more sore.

Amy was the school's best basketball player, and even she was exhausted when they finally got to Quinn's house and knocked on his door. She let out a yawn.

In a scratchy voice, Quinn said...Candy.

And then QUINN OPENED THE DOOR!

"What...but you're...and I'm..."

In a scratchy voice, rubbing his head, Quinn answered. "Hi, Amy. I know it looks bad, but I just got over a cold. Do you have any caramel chocolates for me?"

"But...who is that?"

Amy pointed an accusing finger at the figure in the black robe, who let down the hood to reveal a goopy, brown, monsters face with big yellow rolling eyes and a huge, grinning beak. There was still some caramel stuck to its face. It must have eaten three candy bags worth of caramel while they'd been walking.

"Candy," it grinned, "Good."

This year the kids will be trick-or-treating again. They had to beg for and borrow all of the caramels in the neighborhood, but they made it through until this year.

Maybe they'll even come to YOUR house.

Got any caramels?

THE AUTHOR

MK BELL lives in Niagara, Ontario in a white house with a large dog. Once a year, all sorts of ghouls, goblins, heroes, villains, princesses and ponies show up at her house begging for STUFF....

So once a year, at around midnight, a mysterious typewriter waaaay in the back of her house turns on, and it starts typing...all by itself.

Spooky stories for kids show up right before halloween, and it would be a shame not to share them. After all, that seems to be what the typewriter wants....